Published by Top That! Publishing plc
Tide Mill Way, Woodbridge, Suffolk, IP12 1AP, UK
www.topthatpublishing.com
Text copyright © 2013 Sheri Radford
Illustrations copyright © 2013 Top That! Publishing plc
All rights reserved
0 2 4 6 8 9 7 5 3 1
Printed and bound in China

Creative Director – Simon Couchman
Editorial Director – Daniel Graham

Written by Sheri Radford
Illustrated by Gareth Llewhellin

ISBN 978-1-78244-170-0

A catalogue record for this book is available from the British Library
Printed and bound in China

It's Following Me!

by Sheri Radford

'To Katya and all the other feisty felines who have
left their paw prints on my heart.'
Sheri Radford

It's behind me in the kitchen,
It's behind me in the hall,
It's behind me when I'm leaping,
It's behind me when I fall.

It follows me in the darkness,
It follows me in the sun,
It follows me when I'm feeling sad,
Or when I'm having fun.

It's behind me when I'm sleeping,
It's behind me when I wake,
It's behind me in the garden,
It's behind me by the lake.

It follows me when I'm walking,
Or running down the hall,
It follows me when I'm pouncing,
Or pressed up against the wall.

I wonder why it follows me?
I wonder why it tries?
I need a good detective,
Or several clever spies.

I've tried to ignore it,
I've tried not to stare,
I've tried to pretend,
That I just don't care.

But it's behind me when I'm eating,
It's behind me when I nap,
It's behind me when I'm meowing,
Or when I'm curled up on a lap.

I've tried at times to run away,
I've even tried to flee,
But it seems that everywhere I go,
It always follows me!

It's behind me in the basement,
It's behind me on the stairs,
It's behind me on the sofa,
It's behind me on the chairs.

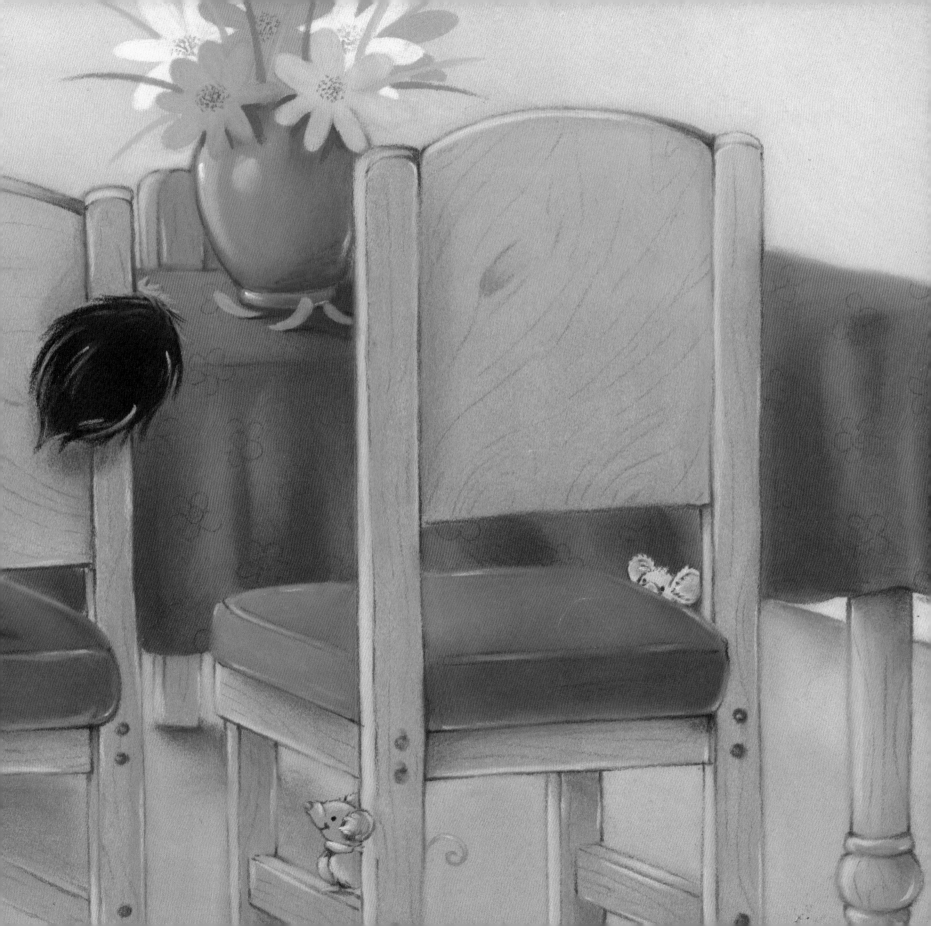

It's really rather funny looking,
Sticking straight up in the air.
It doesn't matter where I go,
It always is right there.

If I remain alert,
And stay on my guard,
Then I'm sure to catch it,
And I'll bite it hard.

Ouch!

More great picture books from Top That! Publishing

ISBN 978-1-78244-064-2

A rhyming storybook, full of nonsense, by inimitable author, Edward Lear.

ISBN 978-1-78244-073-4

This tale, full of fun and folly, recalls the Quangle Wangle and his delightful hat.

ISBN 978-1-84956-778-7

A fantastical tale about a boy and the adventures he has with his rocking horse.

ISBN 978-1-78244-040-6

Follow the little raindrop's adventure and learn all about the water cycle.

ISBN 978-1-78244-059-8

Peter's pebbles come to life in this perfectly crafted tale, full of imagination.

ISBN 978-1-78244-074-1

Cammy the colourful chameleon learns an important lesson in this vibrant tale.

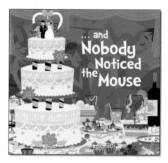

ISBN 978-1-78244-189-2

An enchanting tale about an illusive mouse that nobody notices ... do you?

ISBN 978-1-78244-158-8

A humorous story written in the classic pirate song tradition.

ISBN 978-1-78244-109-0

Search the beautifully illustrated tale to find the hidden ghosts.

ISBN 978-1-78244-187-8

A heartwarming tale about the magic of children's love and creativity.

ISBN 978-1-84956-438-0

A fantastical tale about unruly morning hair and a mischievous fairy.

ISBN 978-1-84956-439-7

The animal food chain is turned upside-down in this funny story with a twist.

Available from all good bookstores or visit www.topthatpublishing.com
Look for Top That! Apps in the Apple iTunes Store